HOW TO USE THIS BOOK

Read the captions in the 31-page booklet, then
turn to the sticker pages and choose the picture
that best fits in the space available.
(Hint: check the sticker labels for helpful clues!)

•

Don't forget that your stickers can be placed on
the page and peeled off again. If you are careful,
you can even use your stickers more than once.

•

There are lots of fantastic extra stickers too!

LONDON, NEW YORK, MELBOURNE,
MUNICH, AND DELHI

Written and edited by Shari Last and Lisa Stock
Designed by Anne Sharples
Cover designed by Jon Hall

First published in the United States in 2011 by
DK Publishing
375 Hudson Street
New York, New York 10014

11 12 13 14 15 10 9 8 7 6 5 4 3
003–178068–02/11

Page design copyright © 2011 Dorling Kindersley Limited

ISBN: 978-0-7566-8254-5

Color reproduction by Alta Image, UK
Printed and bound by
L-Rex Printing Co., Ltd, China

Discover more at
www.dk.com
www.starwars.com

THE FORCE

The Force is a powerful and mysterious energy that flows through all living things. Jedi use the light side of the Force for good and Sith use the dark side for evil. During the Clone Wars, the Republic army is led by the Jedi, while the Sith secretly control their opponents—the Separatist army.

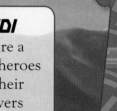

PALPATINE
Chancellor Palpatine is the ruler of the Republic. Secretly he is an evil Sith Lord.

THE JEDI
The Jedi are a group of heroes who use their Force powers to fight for peace and justice.

REPUBLIC
The galaxy is a Republic, which means it is governed by an elected Senate.

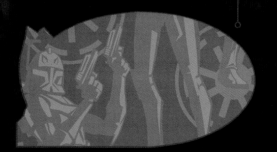

THE SITH
The Sith are secretive villains who try to take over the galaxy using their dark side powers.

SEPARATISTS
The Separatists are prepared to fight to break away from the Republic's rule.

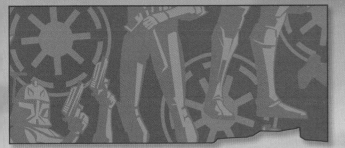

THE CLONE WARS
Republic and Separatist armies battle against each other in the Clone Wars.

LIGHTSABER CRYSTALS
Blue or green crystals are usually used in Jedi lightsaber weapons and are powered by the Force.

CLONE TROOPERS
The Republic army is made up of thousands of identical clone troopers.

BATTLE DROIDS
The Separatist army is made up of millions of battle droids.

RED LIGHTSABER
Sith use artificial crystals in their lightsabers, which glow red.

JEDI COUNCIL
Jedi Generals lead the clone army. They are directed by the Jedi Council.

THE LIGHT SIDE

The Jedi use the light side of the Force to protect the galaxy. They would prefer to be peacekeepers, but in times of war they are prepared to fight. The Jedi serve as Generals in the Clone Wars, during which their Force powers and Jedi values give the Republic an advantage.

BRAVERY
Ahsoka Tano is a trainee Jedi, called a Padawan. She still has much to learn.

STRENGTH
Kit Fisto is an experienced Jedi Master. He is highly skilled with a lightsaber.

FORCE SENSITIVITY
Anakin Skywalker is strong with the Force. He can teach Ahsoka a lot about being a Jedi.

WISDOM
Yoda is known for his knowledge and mastery of the Force.

LOYALTY
Barriss Offee uses the Force for the good of the Galactic Republic.

DIPLOMACY
Obi-Wan Kenobi manages to keep a cool head even during the trickiest conflicts.

LEADERSHIP
Mace Windu is second in command to Yoda. He leads the Jedi in many dangerous battles.

COMPASSION
Jedi General Shaak Ti sees the special qualities inside each and every clone soldier.

OBEDIENCE
Luminara Unduli believes discipline is the most vital Jedi virtue of all.

HONOR
Aayla Secura teaches Ahsoka the importance of sticking to the Jedi's strict rules.

JUSTICE
Plo Koon has a strong sense of right and wrong. He leads his regiment of clone troopers with conviction.

THE DARK SIDE

The dark side of the Force feeds on negative emotions such as fear and hate. It is studied by the Sith and other villains who use the Force to become very powerful and very dangerous. The Sith use their dark side qualities on their quest to take control of the galaxy.

SECRECY
Sith Lord Darth Sidious controls both sides of the Clone Wars, but he conceals his true identity.

AMBITION
Count Dooku is Darth Sidious's Sith apprentice. He leads the Separatists and their droid army.

VENGEANCE
Asajj Ventress is a deadly assassin with Sith powers. She has little conscience and will take revenge on anyone who wrongs her.

POWER-HUNGRY

Poggle the Lesser wants to be more powerful so he works for the Sith. He built the droid army for Dooku.

COWARDICE

Nute Gunray controls most of the trade in the galaxy. He is a coward who takes orders from Darth Sidious.

RAW POWER

The Nightsisters are a clan of witches who use the dark side to gain mystical powers.

GREED

Bounty hunters like Cad Bane and Aurra Sing do not have dark side powers, but they often work for the Sith.

DANGER

Savage Opress is a Dathomirian warrior trained in the dark side by Asajj and Dooku.

HATRED

General Grievous is a vicious cyborg who joins forces with the Sith. He particularly hates Jedi.

TRAINING

The Jedi pass on their Force knowledge from Master to Padawan. During the Clone Wars, the Jedi also help to train the Republic's clone army in the lessons of war. But they had better watch out—the Sith teach their own evil Force powers to others, too!

WANNABES
Clone cadets face tough physical and mental training before they can become Republic soldiers.

EVIL TEACHER
Asajj helps transform Savage into a ferocious monster, who is ready to kill whoever she says.

YOUNGLINGS
Infants who show promise with the Force are trained together by Jedi Masters.

TOUGH TASK
Jedi Shaak Ti has the job of supervising clone training on the planet Kamino.

DARK LESSONS
Dooku has trained Asajj well in lightsaber dueling and Force manipulation.

IDEAL PADAWAN
Barriss has been trained by her Master Luminara to be loyal and trustworthy.

RESPECT
Anakin is no longer Obi-Wan's Padawan, but he can still learn from his old Master.

TEACHING AID
Training droids are used to test the cadets' abilities and prepare them to face real, ruthless Separatist droids.

PEER PRESSURE
Ahsoka is a teacher and role model for students at the Royal Academy of Government on Mandalore.

DIVERSE UNIVERSE

The galaxy is made up of millions of planets and species. Although the Force flows through every living thing, only some beings are able to connect with it and use it. But even those with no Force powers have a part to play in the Clone Wars.

HUTT
Arok the Hutt has bluish-tinged skin and enjoys diamond cigars. He is a member of the Hutt Council.

NIKTO
Ima-Gun Di is a Force-sensitive Nikto from Kintan. Di's powers were noticed early and he became a Jedi.

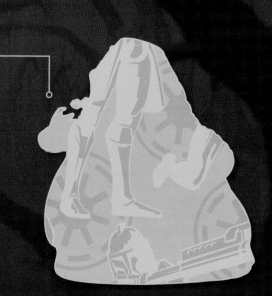

ARCONA
El-Les is a green-skinned Arcona. He helps Jedi Shaak Ti train clone cadets on the planet Kamino.

TOOP
Sha'rellian toops are starfish-like creatures. Mama the Hutt wears toops on her body because she thinks they make her look nicer.

SINITEEN
Bric is a Siniteen with a large, brain-shaped head. He trains clone cadets on Kamino, and isn't afraid to speak his mind!

PA'LOWICK

Sy Snootles is a feisty Pa'lowick singer with bright red lips. She works for Jabba the Hutt.

MOOGAN

Moogans are tall and thin and have green-speckled skin. They often smuggle goods across the galaxy.

TWI'LEK

Ratch is a blue-skinned Twi'lek pirate who travels with a group of Weequay thugs.

DRAGONSNAKE

Dragonsnakes are huge and deadly. Obi-Wan comes across one in the swamps of Nal Hutta.

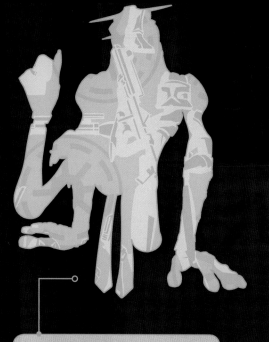

A LIFE OF CRIME
Cassie Cryar is a thief. When she steals a lightsaber, she is choosing to pick a fight with the Jedi.

PROFIT FROM WAR
Doge Nakha Urus supplies fuel to the Republic. But he doesn't always play fair!

MONEY TALKS
For bounty hunter Greedo, the choice is simple: Who will pay the most?

A CHILD'S CHOICE
Boba Fett's father was destroyed by Jedi Mace Windu. Now Boba must decide how much he wants revenge.

FAMILY MAN
Baron Papanoida chooses to rescue his kidnapped daughters himself, rather than join the Separatists.

KATUUNKO
King Katuunko helps the Republic when innocent lives are in danger.

NO MASTER
Trained by Asajj as well as Dooku, Savage surprises everyone when he decides to disobey them both!

TOUGH CHOICES

Jedi and Sith can turn to the Force for help with tricky decisions—but not everyone is so lucky. When choosing sides in the Clone Wars, most people must make the choice without any Force advice: Whose side are they on?

JABBA
Jabba the Hutt controls a lot of trade in the galaxy. Both the Republic and the Separatists want him on their side.

CHOOSING SIDES
Onaconda Farr handed his friend, Padmé Amidala, over to the Separatists—but then he helped her escape.

HONORABLE
The Mandalorian Duchess Satine does not want to choose sides during the Clone Wars.

TEMPTATION
Anakin is often tempted by the dark side. He must resist, but is he strong enough?

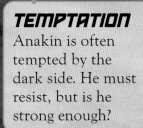

FORCE JUMP

Yoda can leap through the air in battle, which gives him an advantage, despite being so small.

FORCE HEALING

Barriss Offee uses her Force power to heal the sick and injured quickly.

FORCE LIGHTNING

Sith fire deadly, crackling energy from their fingers to shock and burn their victims.

ENERGY WEAPON

Lightsabers are used to their full potential when they are controlled with the Force.

TELEKINESIS

Count Dooku can lift and move very heavy objects just by concentrating on them.

THE FORCE AS A WEAPON

The Force can be channeled by the Jedi and the Sith to gain incredible powers. Force-sensitive beings can use the Force's power to protect themselves and their allies... or to cause their enemies great damage!

FORCE CHOKE
Asajj uses a Force choke to weaken her enemies without even touching them.

JEDI MIND TRICK
Ahsoka uses the Force to persuade a guard into doing just what she wants.

FORCE PILOT
Anakin utilizes his Force skills in the cockpit. He performs daring maneuvers with ease.

FORCE TRACKING
Quinlan Vos's skills as a Force tracker allow him to sense the path that an enemy has taken.

FORCE STEALTH
Palpatine is more skilled than anyone at Force concealment. He hides his dark side loyalty very well.

WEAPONS

Danger is all around. Villains and peace lovers alike must defend themselves from their enemies. The Force is the ultimate weapon for attack or defense. Those without such special powers must seek out a deadly alternative.

LIGHTSABER
Jedi Master Di has perfected his lightsaber skills so he can beat the Sith.

ELECTROSTAFF
MagnaGuards carry lightsaber-resistant staffs to protect General Grievous.

SPEAR
Savage Opress uses ferocious dark side powers to wield his spear.

BLASTER
Clone troopers use DC-15A blasters, which can pierce even heavy armor.

TOXIC DART
The poison inside the Nightsisters' toxic darts dulls enemy senses.

SPA DROID

Spa droids help refresh worn out droids. R2-D2 enjoys his hot oil scrub.

TACTICAL DROID

Tactical droids help Separatist leaders plan and analyze battle strategies.

INTERROGATION

Interrogation droids are vicious and cruel. J0-N0 tries to get secret data from C-3PO.

BAKER DROID

No one in the galaxy can make a jogan fruit cake as well as a baker droid!

BATTLING

Separatist battle droids have many functions, but they can't think for themselves.

ASTROMECH

Astromech droids navigate and repair starships. R2-D2 plugs into Anakin's starship and helps him in times of danger.

TRIDENT DRILL

Trident drills soar through the air and drill their way into buildings —where they deploy aqua droids!

BETRAYAL

Is anyone in the galaxy exactly what they seem? Everyone appears to be keeping a secret. During the Clone Wars, Jedi and Sith must use their Force senses to work out who they can trust... and who they can't!

SECRET LOVE
Anakin has betrayed a Jedi vow! He secretly married Senator Padmé Amidala.

CHARMER
The Jedi suspect former Senator Rush Clovis of being a traitor.

JILTED
Sy Snootles was heartbroken when Ziro the Hutt left her. She wants revenge... so she attacks Ziro!

TEMPTING
Anakin thinks that Palpatine is his friend. But he is deceived.

DECEIT
Chancellor Palpatine is plotting to take control of the entire galaxy.

TROOPER TRAITOR
Clone trooper Slick really hates his Jedi commanders. He passes secret information to Asajj to get back at them.

TRICKY TALE
Mother Talzin tricks Dooku into taking on a new assassin—who is really working against him!

BRIBED
Captain Argyus is an Elite Republic Commando. He is being paid by Dooku to betray his comrades.

UNDERCOVER
R3-S6 looks like a friend of the Jedi, but he has been reprogrammed to spy for Grievous.

REVENGE
It's a bad idea for Dooku to betray Asajj—he's the one who taught her to master the dark side!

RESCUE

The Clone Wars bring constant danger to the galaxy. When innocent lives are threatened, Jedi and non-Jedi heroes charge to the rescue! They use every power, talent, and skill at their disposal to defeat their enemies and make the galaxy a safer place.

HUTTLET
Rotta is Jabba the Hutt's young son. When he is kidnapped by the Separatists, Anakin and Ahsoka rescue him.

ROBOT RESCUE
Medical droids treat injured Jedi and soldiers so they can return to battle.

SAVING LIVES
Jedi Master Saesee Tiin plays a crucial role in the rescue of Jedi and clone troopers from the planet Lola Sayu.

STARFIGHTER MISSION
Plo Koon is a skilled Jedi pilot. He leads a daring mission to rescue stranded Jedi.

PROTECT AND SERVE
Ahsoka protects Senator Padmé Amidala from danger.

PEACEFUL WARRIOR

Mace wants peace in the galaxy more than anything—but that doesn't mean he won't combat evil.

OUTFOXED

Clone Commander Fox is a Coruscant guard. When Padmé Amidala is held hostage, Fox rushes to the scene.

USE THE FORCE

Ahsoka uses a Jedi mind trick to locate a kidnapped Senator, Chi Eekway.

FLYING FRIEND

A gentle, flying creature called an aiwha rescues Obi-Wan from underwater trouble.

SACRIFICE

Jedi Master Di holds off hordes of deadly battle droids while terrified Twi'lek families escape to safety.

SPEEDING

Traveling around the galaxy is fast-paced and exciting. Selecting the right ship, starfighter, submarine, or speeder can make or break a mission. Some vehicles can travel even faster than usual if their pilot has Force powers.

FANBLADE
Asajj's starfighter zips through space at high speeds thanks to its huge solar sail fan.

PANTORAN CRUISER
Baron Papanoida's official cruiser may be small, but it is fast and comfortable.

GOZANTI FREIGHTER
Cargo freighters are large, safe transport ships that carry goods across the galaxy.

JEDI STARFIGHTER
The Delta-7B is the starship of choice for the Jedi. It can be controlled using the Force.

NIGHTSPEEDER
Asajj borrows a speeder from her Nightsister clan.

DROID TRI-FIGHTER

Separatist fighter droids fly straight into battle—they don't even need a pilot to steer them!

MOOGAN SMUGGLERS

This ship is big enough to fill with smuggled goods. It has six 'legs' that can walk around once the ship has landed.

SWAMP SPEEDER

Ziro the Hutt and Sy Snootles use this speeder for traveling through the Nal Hutta swamps.

FIGHTING FOR BALANCE

The Clone Wars are waged in fierce battles of all sizes. Huge armies of clones and droids clash, while Jedi and Sith warriors use their Force powers—and blazing lightsabers—in tense duels. Who will win?

LIGHT VS. DARK
Anakin must focus all his Jedi powers when he fights Asajj, as her dark side skills are strong.

CYBORG DUEL
Obi-Wan and General Grievous are old enemies. They meet again for another duel.

ONE VS. TWO
Savage uses a deadly double-bladed lightsaber to fight two Jedi at once!

FLYING FIGHT
Cad Bane might have rocket boots, but Obi-Wan can Force jump even higher!

HIS OWN MASTER
Savage defies both of his former Masters when he takes on Count Dooku and Asajj Ventress.

CLONE ARMY

Clone troopers are sent to planets across the galaxy to defend the Republic from the Separatists.

SITH POWER

Asajj uses her dual lightsabers and all her dark side powers in a duel with Obi-Wan and Anakin.

INVISIBLE ENEMY

Asajj uses her new Nightsister powers to become almost invisible.

BOUNTY HUNTER VS. PADAWAN

Ahsoka's Jedi skills are put to the test when she battles against Aurra Sing.

DROID ARMY

Droids attack in such huge numbers, it is almost impossible to stop them!

UNEXPECTED HEROES

Not every hero is a Jedi Knight with amazing powers. The Force can be a useful weapon, but sometimes honor and courage are just as powerful. Many Republic soldiers and Jedi warriors have been saved by unexpected heroes.

FIGHTING FOR FREEDOM
Cham Syndulla is a Twi'lek freedom fighter. He will do anything to save his people.

OLD CLONE
Ninety-Nine was rejected by the clone army, but he saves many lives on Kamino.

PERFORMING
Jar Jar Binks saves the day! He causes a distraction so a ship full of emergency supplies can depart in safety.

SEPARATIST
Mina Bonteri is a Separatist who joins Padmé on a quest for peace.

CLEVER R2
R2-D2 exceeds his astromech duties when he saves Anakin from a crash.

DETECTIVE

Cadet Korkie does not let age stand in his way! The youngster helps Ahsoka uncover a deadly plot.

SENSE OF HONOR

Sugi is a bounty hunter who defends her clients, even when her own life is at risk.

A SENATOR STRIKES

Padmé Amidala fires a deadly shot from her ion blaster to save Ahsoka from Aurra Sing.

FAMILY FRIEND

Senator Riyo Chuchi shows courage when she helps rescue Baron Papanoida's kidnapped family.

31

KNOWLEDGE IS POWER

For centuries the Jedi have used their sharp wits and Force intuition to collect knowledge about the galaxy. To succeed on any mission, it is vital to gather all the facts first. But having valuable knowledge can sometimes be risky!

DROIDNAPPED
Cad Bane kidnaps C-3PO to steal the knowledge stored inside his head.

ANALYSIS
Detailed scientific tests help to uncover a secret and evil plot.

WAR ROOM
Jedi use Holocrons to store priceless information from around the galaxy.

TEMPLE LIBRARY
Ahsoka studies in the Jedi Temple library. It stores a vast collection of Jedi wisdom.

FOE OR FRIEND?
Lux Bonteri is a Separatist. He helps Ahsoka understand the other side of the conflict.

MEDITATION
Jedi use the Force to focus their minds. This helps them make very wise decisions.

DATA CONTAINER
A holodiary stores information, which can be valuable to enemies.

Peer Pressure

Younglings

ARF
Trooper

Bravery

Detective

Force Sensitivity

Jedi
Starfighter

Droid
Tri-Fighter

Meditation

Moogan
Smugglers

Old Clone

Saving
Lives

Performing

Diplomacy

Compassion

Separatist

Evil Teacher

Captain
Keeli

Data
Container

Huttlet

Respect

Clone Pilot

Force
Healing

Honor

Protect
and Serve

Special
Ops

Dark
Lessons

ARC
Trooper

Nightspeeder

Droidnapped

Obedience

Starfighter
Mission

Clone
Trooper

Force Choke

Outfoxed

Foe or
Friend?

Ideal Padawan

War Room

Force Stealth

Telekinesis

Force Pilot

Temple
Library

Robot
Rescue

Force
Lightning

Force Tracking

Wannabes

Pantoran
Cruiser

Analysis

Justice

Gozanti Freighter

Cadet

Loyalty

Energy
Weapon

Sacrifice

Leadership

Peaceful
Warrior

Jedi Generals

Commander
Wolffe

Use
the Force

Family
Friend

Fanblade

Kamino
ARF

Swamp
Speeder

Teaching Aid

Jedi Mind Trick

A Senator
Strikes

Sense of
Honor

Wisdom

Fighting for
Freedom

Flying
Friend

Tough Task

Fixer

Strength

Leaders

Force
Jump

Clever
R2

Profit
from War

Police
Power

Spa Droid

Protocol

Flying
Fight

Toxic
Dart

Death
Ball

Vengeance

Tricky Tale

Spear

Clone Troopers

Rifles

Republic

Arcona

The Sith

Bounty Hunter Vs. Padawan

Ambition

Tempting

Dragonsnake

Hatred

The Jedi

Electrostaff

Choosing Sides

Invisible Enemy

Separatists

Astromech

Lightsaber Crystals

Weequay Blaster

Assassin

His Own Master

Clone
Army

Trooper
Traitor

No
Master

Hutt

Katuunko

Secrecy

Trident Drill

Aqua Droid

Toop

Bribed

Cowardice

Danger

Greed

Baker Droid

Undercover

Sith Power

The Clone Wars

Siniteen

Nikto

Night
Stick

Twi'lek

Fire!

Jedi
Council

Family Man

Secret
Love

A Life of
Crime

Cyborg Duel

Jilted

Money Talks

Blaster

Pa'lowick

Honorable

Palpatine

Light Vs.
Dark

Charmer

Droid
Army

Battling

One Vs. Two

Raw
Power

Tactical
Droid

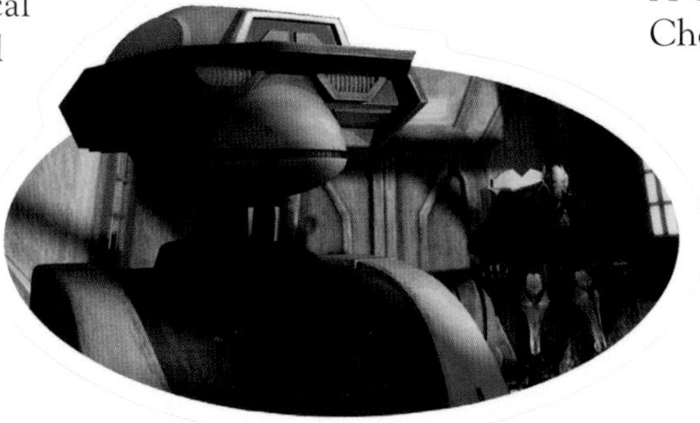

A Child's
Choice

Temptation

Battle
Droids

Demolition

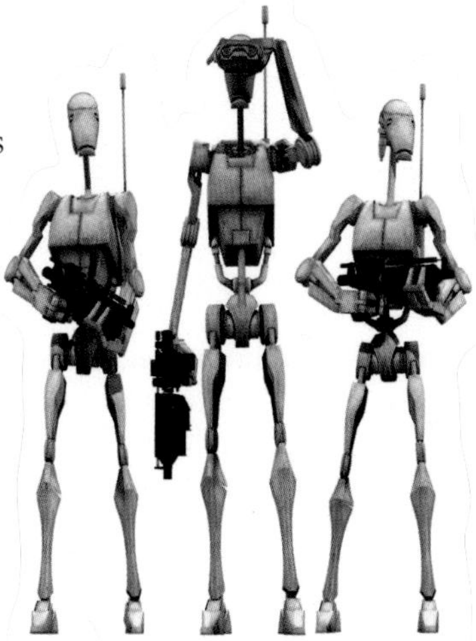

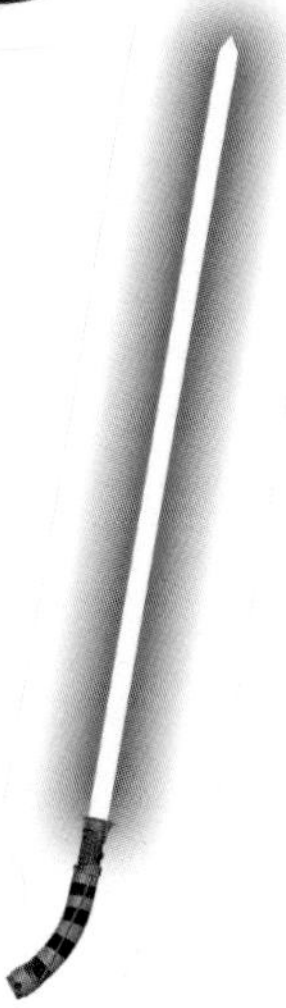

Moogan

Lightsaber

Red Lightsaber

Revenge

Power-
Hungry

Interrogation

Jabba

Deceit

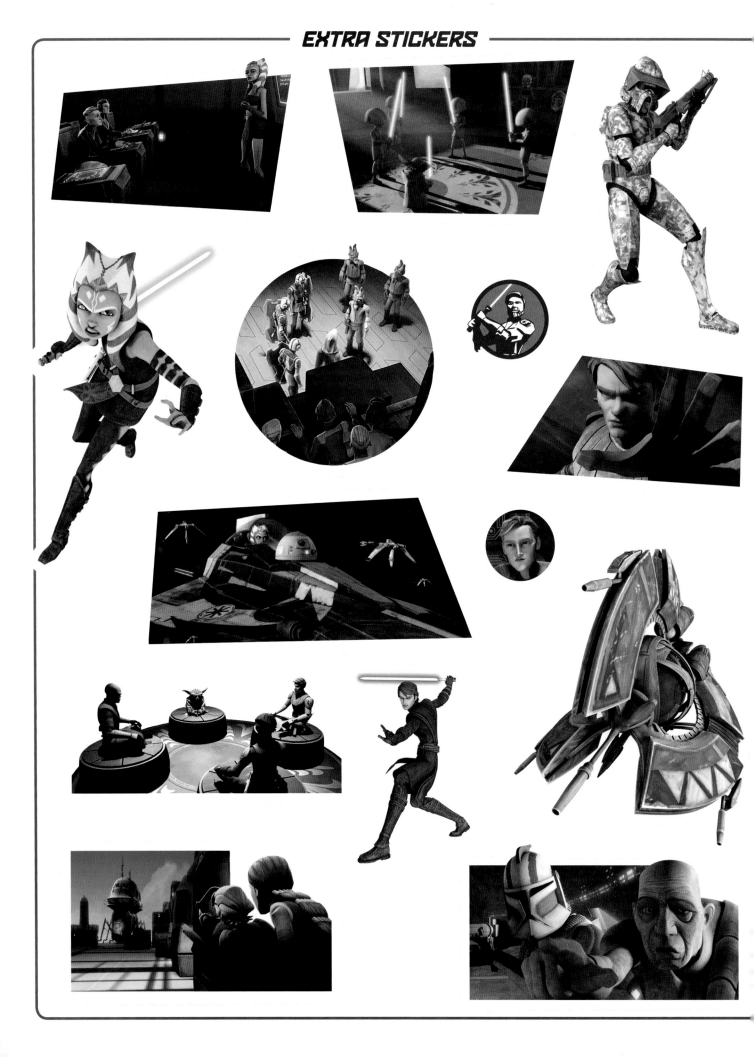